LOUISE
LOVES
ART

For Maggie, my masterpiece

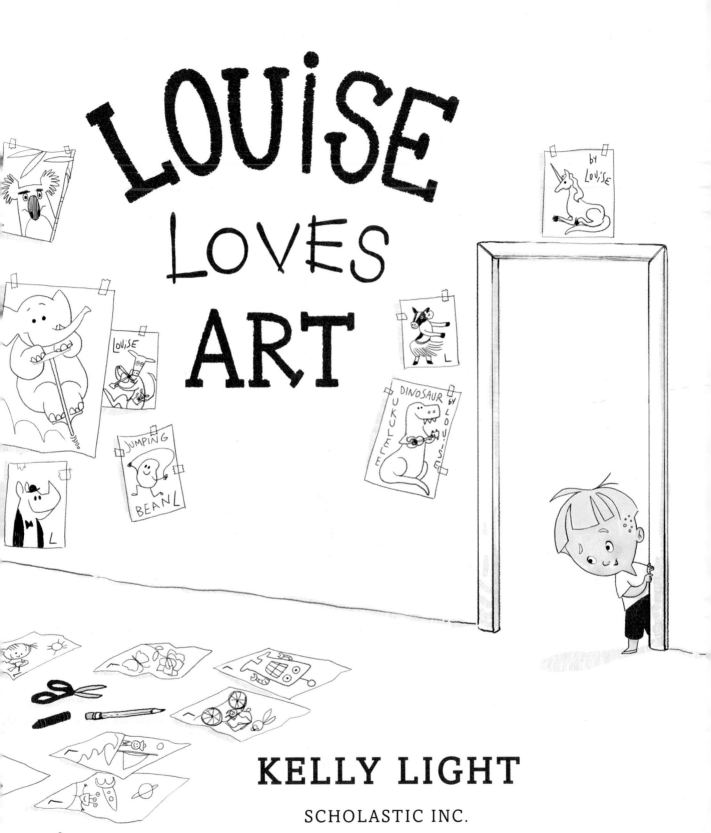

LOUISE LOVES ART

KELLY LIGHT

SCHOLASTIC INC.

I love art!
It's my imagination on the outside.

So little time, so much to draw.
One of these drawings will be my masterpiece—
the greatest drawing I have ever done!

To be a great artist, you have to notice everything.

Every line . . .

every curve . . .

Wait—hold that pose! I will capture your cat-ness!

I've done it.
So fierce! So feline! So fantastic . . .
a masterpiece!

Louise?

Not now, Art. I have to get ready for my show.

PORTRAIT OF A YOUNG ARTISTE

I have to hang each picture just so. . . .

LOUISE

Louise?

It's my pièce de résistance!
I know the perfect spot for it.

The Gallery du Fridge!

LOUISE!

It's my drawing . . .

my masterpiece!

Sorry.

Oh, Art. I love it.

It's your masterpiece.
And I know the perfect spot for it.

Voilà!

ISBN 978-0-545-88788-5

12 11 10 9 8 7 6 5 4 3 2 1   15 16 17 18 19 20/0

Printed in the U.S.A.   08

First Scholastic printing, September 2015

The artist used many black Prismacolor pencils and Photoshop to create the illustrations for this book.
Typography by Alison Donalty

SCHOLASTIC

www.scholastic.com

ISBN 978-0-545-91281-5

$5.99 US

50599

EAN

9 780545 912815